Other books by Patricia Reilly Giff
you will enjoy:

THE LINCOLN LIONS BAND BOOKS:
illustrated by Emily Arnold McCully

MEET THE LINCOLN LIONS BAND

YANKEE DOODLE DRUMSTICKS

THE "JINGLE BELLS" JAM

THE POLKA DOT PRIVATE EYE BOOKS:
illustrated by Blanche Sims

THE MYSTERY OF THE BLUE RING

THE RIDDLE OF THE RED PURSE

THE SECRET AT THE POLK STREET SCHOOL

THE POWDER PUFF PUZZLE

THE CASE OF THE COOL-ITCH KID

GARBAGE JUICE FOR BREAKFAST

THE TRAIL OF THE SCREAMING TEENAGER

THE CLUE AT THE ZOO

YEARLING BOOKS are designed especially to entertain and enlighten young people. Patricia Reilly Giff, consultant to this series, received her bachelor's degree from Marymount College and a master's degree in history from St. John's University. She holds a Professional Diploma in Reading and a Doctorate of Humane Letters from Hofstra University. She was a teacher and reading consultant for many years, and is the author of numerous books for young readers.

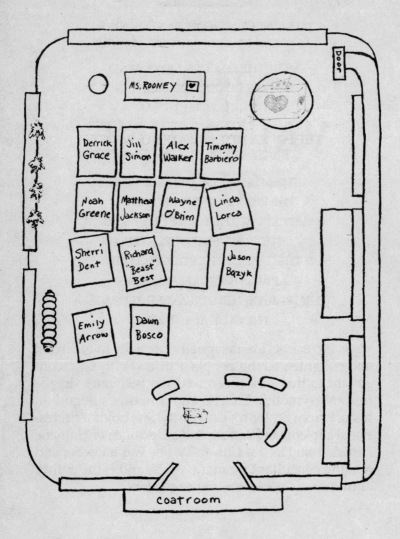

The Kids of the Polk Street School

6

THE VALENTINE STAR

Patricia Reilly Giff

Illustrated by Blanche Sims

A YEARLING BOOK

With love to Therese Rooney

Published by
Bantam Doubleday Dell Books for Young Readers
a division of
Bantam Doubleday Dell Publishing Group, Inc.
1540 Broadway
New York, New York 10036

ISBN: 0-440-49204-1

Printed in the United States of America

February 1985

33   32   31   30   29   28   27

OPM

Chapter 1

Emily Arrow raced across the schoolyard.

"Come on, Uni," she said. She held the little rubber unicorn up high.

She jumped over a clump of snow.

"Faster," she yelled. "Faster."

"Wait up," said a voice behind her.

"Fastest in the world," Emily said.

"Hey," said the voice.

Emily looked back. It was Sherri Dent.

"How about playing something?" Sherri yelled.

Emily shook her head. She wanted to run with Uni.

She raced to the highest snow pile. It was the one near the schoolyard fence.

They weren't supposed to climb on it.

But she was running fast. Too fast to stop.

She galloped to the top of the pile.

Then she raced down again.

Just then Ms. Rooney blew her whistle.

Recess was over.

Emily dashed across the yard to her line.

Sherri Dent was there ahead of her. She stuck her tongue out at Emily.

Her tongue was as pointy as her face.

Emily stared at her.

She opened her mouth.

Then she closed it with a pop.

"Fish face to you, Sherri Dent," Emily said to herself.

Sherri's hand shot up in the air.

"Let's hurry," said Ms. Rooney. "I have a surprise."

"Ms. Rooney," said Sherri. "Emily was playing on the snow pile."

Ms. Rooney frowned at Emily.

Emily ducked her head. She hated it when Ms. Rooney frowned.

2

Ms. Rooney led the line toward the door.

Emily poked her head around Jason Bazyk.

She could see Sherri in front of the line.

Too bad she wasn't closer.

She'd like to give Sherri a kick in the shins.

She'd like to pinch her skinny neck that looked like a pole.

Inside Emily hung up her jacket quickly.

She put Uni inside her desk.

"Is everybody ready?" asked Ms. Rooney.

Emily sat up straight. She remembered Ms. Rooney's surprise.

"This is February tenth," Ms. Rooney said. "Who can tell us what happens in four days?"

Dawn Bosco raised her hand. So did Emily.

"Dawn?" asked Ms. Rooney.

"Valentine's Day," said Dawn.

"Right," said Ms. Rooney.

Ms. Rooney pulled out a box from underneath her desk. It was covered with shiny pink paper. It had a big red heart on it.

4

"This is our Valentine mailbox," said Ms. Rooney. "I'll leave it in front of the room."

Emily raised her hand again. "Are we going to make Valentine cards?"

Ms. Rooney smiled. "We've worked hard on rhyming words. We'll make cards with poems."

"I know a poem," Matthew Jackson said. "Roses are red. Violets are blue. If I were you I'd go to a zoo."

Everyone laughed. Even Ms. Rooney.

"I know one too," Dawn said. "You are the best. Of all the rest."

"I think she means me," Emily's friend Richard Best said. He made believe he was falling out of his seat.

"I did not," said Dawn. Her face was red. "I said it because it rhymes."

Emily laughed. Richard was a funny boy. Everyone called him Beast.

"You'll make wonderful cards," said Ms. Rooney. "But don't sign your names."

"Just 'Guess Who,' " Emily said.

"Right," said Ms. Rooney.

Next to Emily, Dawn took out her pencil box.

Dawn had the best pencil box in the class.

"I have a box of stick-on stars," Dawn whispered. "I'm going to make a great card for Ms. Rooney."

Emily looked out the window.

She wished she had some stick-on stars.

The kind Dawn had. Red and green and gold and silver.

Dawn was a lucky girl.

Dawn pushed the box over toward Emily. "Take some."

Dawn was really a nice girl, Emily thought. She reached for the box.

She took four red stars and two gold ones.

Sherri Dent looked back at Emily and Dawn.

She raised her hand. "I can't think with all this noise," she told Ms. Rooney.

Ms. Rooney shook her head at Emily and Dawn.

6

Emily waited for Ms. Rooney to sit down at her desk.

Then she stared at Sherri.

She couldn't wait for Sherri to turn around.

She'd make a fish face at her.

She'd stick out her tongue and cross her eyes.

While Emily waited she took out paper.

She'd draw a Valentine card for Mrs. Paris, the reading teacher.

She'd put a nice red star on top.

Chapter 2

After lunch Ms. Rooney pointed to a picture.

"This is Abraham Lincoln," she said.

Emily looked at Abraham Lincoln. He had on a big black hat.

"He was a president," Linda Lorca said.

"Right," said Ms. Rooney. "His birthday is February twelfth."

Emily could see that her friend Richard was drawing a picture of Abraham Lincoln.

"Who can tell us more?" Ms. Rooney asked.

"He's on a penny," Wayne O'Brien said.

"What about his life?" asked Ms. Rooney.

Timothy Barbiero put his hand up.

Emily wished she could put her hand up too.

But she didn't know one thing about Abraham Lincoln.

Just then the door opened.

It was Mr. Mancina, the principal. "May I see you a minute?" he asked Ms. Rooney.

"Finish your boardwork," Ms. Rooney told the class.

Everyone sat up straight.

Emily tried to sit up straighter than everyone else.

She hoped Ms. Rooney would call on her to be the monitor.

Ms. Rooney looked around. "Emily," she said.

Emily rushed up to the front of the room.

Ms. Rooney pointed to the chalk on her desk. "If anyone is not doing his work," she said, "write his name down."

Ms. Rooney went outside.

Emily looked around at everyone.

The whole class was working.

All except for Matthew Jackson.

He was playing with his pencil.

He dropped it on the floor.

It rolled under Beast's desk.

Matthew leaned out of his seat to get it.

Emily thought about putting his name on the board. But Matthew wasn't really fooling around.

Emily sat down at Ms. Rooney's desk.

It was a wonderful feeling to be sitting there.

She picked up Ms. Rooney's pen.

She made a little check mark on a piece of paper.

Maybe she'd be a teacher when she grew up.

It was probably a lot of fun. Easy too.

She looked back at the library corner.

If she were a teacher she'd have lots of good books in the classroom.

She spotted a big blue book.

It had a picture of Abraham Lincoln on the cover.

Maybe it would tell about Abraham Lincoln's life.

She stood up. She'd look through the book. She'd know all about Abraham Lincoln by the time Ms. Rooney came back.

Just then Sherri stood up too.

"You're not supposed to—" Emily began.

"I have to get something from the library corner," Sherri said.

Emily looked at the big blue book.

She hoped Sherri wasn't looking at the big blue book too.

"What do you have to get?" Emily asked.

Sherri didn't answer.

She was hurrying over to the library corner.

Emily rushed down the aisle.

She got to the library corner a second ahead of Sherri.

She grabbed the big blue book.

Sherri pulled the book away from her.

"Hey," Emily said.

Sherri raced back to her seat with it.

"You're supposed to be doing boardwork," Emily said.

But Sherri didn't answer.

She was looking at the big blue book.

12

Emily wanted to race down to Sherri's seat.

She wanted to take the big blue book away from her.

She went back to Ms. Rooney's desk.

Then she saw the piece of chalk.

She went to the blackboard. She wrote *Sherri D.* in big white letters.

The chalk screeched across the board.

But Sherri wasn't paying attention. She was still reading the big blue book.

She was going to know all about Abraham Lincoln.

And Emily wasn't going to know anything.

Not one thing.

Chapter 3

The class was quiet when Ms. Rooney opened the door.

"I'm proud of you," she said. "You can hear a pin drop in here."

She looked at the blackboard. "Oh, dear," she said. "Not everyone was working."

Ms. Rooney went to her desk. "Thank you, Emily. You may go back to your seat."

Then Ms. Rooney frowned. "I'm disappointed in you, Sherri," she said.

Emily went down the aisle to her seat.

She took a quick look at Sherri.

Sherri's face was red. She looked as if she were going to cry.

"Time to write our spelling words," said Ms. Rooney. "Three times."

Emily took out her spelling book.

Ms. Rooney looked up again. "As soon as you're finished we have things to talk about."

Emily wrote the first word. "Bean," she said under her breath. "B-e-a-n."

She wondered what Ms. Rooney was going to talk about. Maybe she was going to talk about Sherri.

Emily wrote *bean* three times. "Bean, dean, fean, green," she whispered.

Mean, she thought. Mean to Sherri.

Quickly she wrote the next word. S-t-e-a-m.

She didn't want to think about being mean to Sherri.

Then Sherri stood up. She took the pass for the girls' room. She went outside.

"I have some exciting news," Ms. Rooney said.

Everyone sat up straight.

"We are getting a student teacher," said Ms. Rooney.

"Neat," said Dawn.

This was really exciting news, Emily thought.

The first grade had had a student teacher all year.

Her name was Ms. Martin.

She wore purple nail polish and gold eyeliner.

Emily hoped their student teacher would be just like Ms. Martin.

"When is she coming?" Dawn Bosco asked.

"Tomorrow," said Ms. Rooney.

Good, thought Emily. She'd wear her almost-new yellow blouse. The one with the green kittens on the collar.

The new student teacher would love it.

Dawn leaned over. "I have a brand new sweat suit," she said. "Purple stripes. I think I'll wear it tomorrow."

Emily tried to smile at Dawn. "Nice," she said.

"I'll wear my ladybug earrings too," Dawn said.

16

Emily looked out the window.

That Dawn was the luckiest girl in the world, she thought.

She looked toward the door.

Just then Sherri opened her classroom door. Her eyes looked red.

She walked past Emily's desk.

She dropped a piece of paper on top.

Emily picked it up.

She opened it carefully under her desk so Ms. Rooney wouldn't see.

In big black letters Sherri had written:

YOU'LL BE SORRY.

Chapter 4

The next morning Emily wore her look-like-real fur jacket.

Underneath she had on her yellow blouse.

It had green kittens on the collar.

She wanted to look perfect for the new student teacher.

She rushed down the hall with Richard.

Sherri Dent was ahead of them.

"Come on, Beast," Emily said.

She quick-stepped to get ahead of Sherri.

Sherri looked over her shoulder.

She began to quick-step too.

She dashed into the classroom.

Emily dashed into the classroom right behind her.

"Everyone's in a hurry today," Ms. Rooney said.

Someone was standing next to Ms. Rooney.

It had to be the new student teacher.

She didn't look anything like Ms. Martin.

She didn't have long purple nails.

She didn't have gold eyeliner.

She didn't have any eyeliner at all.

She was wearing a puffy pink coat. And she was ten times prettier than Ms. Martin.

Emily took off her look-like-real fur jacket.

She straightened her blouse.

She hoped the new student teacher would see the kittens on the collar.

"This is Ms. Vincent," Ms. Rooney said.

"Wow," said Matthew Jackson.

Ms. Vincent smiled at him.

"Ms. Vincent will sit with you this morning," said Ms. Rooney. "She has to get to know everyone."

Ms. Vincent took off her puffy pink coat. She hung it in Ms. Rooney's closet.

Then she sat in an empty chair near the science table.

"Time to work, class," said Ms. Rooney. "You can talk with Ms. Vincent when you finish your boardwork."

Quickly Emily took out her pencil. She'd try to be the first one finished.

She was dying to talk to Ms. Vincent.

She was dying to tell her about the Valentine box.

She opened her notebook.

Inside was the **You'll be sorry** note from Sherri Dent.

Emily had forgotten she had put it there.

She looked at Sherri Dent.

She wondered how Sherri was going to make her sorry.

She crumpled up the note.

She shoved it into her desk.

She wasn't going to spoil her day.

She wasn't going to think about that mean Sherri.

21

She wasn't even going to look at her.

Emily looked up at the board. She had to do health. Fill in the blanks.

Emily hated health.

She never knew the exact right answer.

She wrote the first sentence.

Take a bath ____ times a week.

She closed her eyes.

Her mother made her take a bath every day.

Six. No, seven times a week.

Ms. Vincent looked clean. Very clean.

Emily opened her eyes.

She wrote 13 in the blank.

That should be enough baths for anybody.

She copied the next sentence quickly.

Drink ____ glasses of water every day.

She tried to think of how many glasses of water she drank.

She drank one when she was brushing her teeth. But that didn't count. It was only a swallow.

She thought for a long time.

She didn't drink any water.

No. Sometimes she did. When she wanted to get out of the classroom, she'd . . .

She looked out the window. Sometimes it helped her to think. She heard Sherri say, "Easy. Simple."

Emily looked down at her paper. How many glasses of water?

Maybe two.

She took a little peek at Dawn's paper.

Dawn had written 6.

Six glasses of water every day.

Too much. You'd probably be ready to drown.

Emily erased her 2. She wrote 4.

More than two, but less than six.

Probably just right.

She looked up. Sherri Dent was staring at her.

Emily's face felt hot.

"I think someone is cheating," Sherri said.

"I hope no one is looking at anyone else's work," said Ms. Rooney.

Emily ducked her head.

That Sherri Dent, she thought. She was getting to be the biggest tattletale in the world.

Emily hoped Ms. Vincent didn't think she was a cheater. She certainly wasn't a cheater.

She erased 4 and put 2 back on her paper.

She started the third sentence.

Name two yellow vegetables.

She knelt up a little. Sherri had turned her paper over. She was writing fast.

Emily tried to think fast too.

Two yellow vegetables. Corn, of course.

She could think of string beans, and lettuce.

Too bad Ms. Rooney hadn't asked about green vegetables.

Maybe Ms. Rooney had made a mistake.

Maybe there weren't any more yellow vegetables.

Maybe she should tell Ms. Rooney.

Ms. Vincent would think she was very smart.

She raised her hand.

"Yes, Emily," Ms. Rooney said.

"I think there's a mistake," Emily said.

"Really?"

"Didn't you mean to say, 'Name one yellow vegetable'?" Emily asked.

Ms. Rooney shook her head.

"I don't think . . ." Emily began.

Matthew turned around. "Don't you know any more?"

Emily felt her face get hot. She wondered if Ms. Vincent thought she was the dumbest kid in the class.

Just then Sherri Dent shot past her.

She went straight to Ms. Vincent's seat.

"I'm all finished," she said. "I wrote three yellow vegetables."

"Wonderful," said Ms. Vincent.

Emily tore a piece of paper out of her notebook. She wrote:

I'm going to get you.

She folded it four times. Then she tossed it toward Sherri's desk.

It landed on Sherri's chair.

Good, Emily thought. She swallowed.

She hoped she wasn't going to cry in front of everybody.

Chapter 5

The next morning Emily went straight to the Valentine box. She slipped in three cards.

One for Dawn Bosco. One for Beast. And one for Timothy.

She still had a pile of cards to do.

She was going to make a card for everyone.

Everyone but Sherri Dent.

Emily went to the coatroom. Sherri was there too.

Emily made a little sniffing sound.

She hung up her jacket. Then she went to her seat.

She folded a piece of looseleaf into fours. It would make a nice Valentine card.

She picked up her red crayon and wrote:

Ms. Vincent is not mean.
She looks like a dream.

She put a red star on top.

Ms. Vincent would love it.

Ms. Rooney would love it too.

Emily had used two of her spelling words.

On the bottom she wrote:

Guess Who

She dashed up to the Valentine box and dropped it in.

Just then the door opened.

It was the office monitor. "Please bring the attendance to the office," she said to Ms. Rooney.

"Right away," Ms. Rooney said. She looked at Ms. Vincent. "Are you ready to give your lesson?"

Ms. Vincent went to the front of the room. "Boys and girls," she said.

Emily saw that no one was paying attention.

29

She sat up straight. She hoped Ms. Vincent would see.

Matthew and Beast were playing "got you last."

Dawn was making a Valentine card for Mr. Mancina.

It had about fifty green stars all over it.

Ms. Rooney clapped her hands.

Everyone stopped what he was doing.

"We are going to learn about February birthdays," said Ms. Vincent.

She spoke in a little voice.

Emily could hardly hear her.

Ms. Rooney walked to the door. "Ms. Vincent," she said. "Please speak a little louder." She went out.

In front of Emily, Beast and Matthew were punching each other again.

Ms. Vincent cleared her throat. "Who knows a famous birthday in February?"

Everyone raised hands.

Matthew stopped punching Beast.

30

He raised his hand too.

"Yes, Michael," Ms. Vincent said.

Everybody laughed.

"Matthew," someone said.

Ms. Vincent ducked her head a little. "I'm sorry. Matthew."

Emily looked over toward the window. Sherri was waving her hand hard. She was holding the big blue book.

Emily hoped Ms. Vincent wouldn't see her.

Matthew stood up. "A famous February person."

"Yes," said Ms. Vincent.

"My grandfather," Matthew said. "Devoe Jackson."

"De-vooooe," Timothy Barbiero said. "I never heard of a name like that."

Everybody started to laugh again.

Ms. Vincent said, "That's not very kind."

"He wasn't famous, I bet," said Jason.

"He was famous in our family," Matthew said. "He had three cars."

Emily looked over at Sherri.

Sherri was waving her hand even harder.

"Who can tell us another one?" Ms. Vincent asked.

Dawn Bosco raised her hand. "William Henry Harrison."

Ms. Vincent blinked. "Wonderful."

"Is that your grandfather?" Beast asked.

Dawn shook her head. "No, he was a president. My Aunt Olga told me. Her birthday was the other day. It's the same day as his. February ninth."

Suddenly Emily remembered. She raised her hand. "George Washington," she called out.

"Good," said Ms. Vincent.

"I know about his life too," said Emily. "I don't even need a big blue book."

"The whole world knows about George Washington," said Sherri.

"He was our first president," said Ms. Vincent.

"I know all about Abraham Lincoln," said

Sherri. "They called him Honest Abe. He was our sixteenth president."

Sherri looked at Emily.

She made a pointy know-it-all face.

"His birthday is today," Sherri said.

"That's pretty good," said Beast.

"Neat," said Ms. Vincent.

Emily slid down in her seat.

She felt like banging Sherri on the head with a book. A big blue book.

Chapter 6

When Ms. Rooney came back, they started board-work.

It was math, Emily's best subject.

Emily drew nine sticks on her paper.

She crossed out four of them.

She began to count. "Nine take away four is . . ."

Up in front, Ms. Rooney was counting too.

"Thirty . . . thirty-one . . ." Ms. Rooney said.

She was adding up the lunch money.

Emily put a big five on her paper.

She waited for Ms. Rooney to call her name.

Emily was the lunch-money monitor for February.

It was the best job in the classroom.

"Emily Arrow," said Ms. Rooney.

Emily rushed up to Ms. Rooney's desk. She took the brown lunch-money envelope.

Jill Simon, her lunch partner, was absent.

Emily looked around the classroom.

She looked at Sherri. She made a little face.

Sherri made a face back at her.

Then Emily looked at Richard.

He was drawing a picture. It looked like a fat gray groundhog.

He had been drawing pictures of groundhogs since Groundhog Day.

"I pick Beast," Emily said.

Ms. Rooney nodded.

Richard put down his crayon. He stood up.

Quickly they went down the hall.

"I'm glad you picked me," Richard said.

"I'm glad too," said Emily.

"I thought you were going to pick Sherri Dent," Richard said.

"Never," Emily said.

"She's pretty smart," Richard said. "She knows all about Abraham Lincoln."

Emily walked a little faster. "She's a know-it-all. She's a tattletale know-it-all. She's a pointy-face tattletale. . . ."

"She's a pretty nice kid," Beast said. "She gave me a candy bar last week. For nothing."

Emily thought for a moment. "She used to be." She frowned. "But not anymore."

They went into the cafeteria.

The cafeteria lady was waiting for them.

She took the lunch-money envelope.

Emily and Richard went back into the hall.

They stopped at the side doors. They looked out at the piles of snow.

"It's hot in here," Emily said.

"Boiling," Richard said.

Emily pushed open the door a crack.

She poked her nose out. "Smell that air."

Richard took a sniff. "Neat," he said.

"Wouldn't you love to go outside?" Emily asked.

"Just to run down the path and back," Richard said.

37

"We'd get in trouble if someone saw us," Emily said.

"We could go fast," Richard said.

"Go like a rocket ship," said Emily.

She took another breath of cold air. "Ready?"

"Go," said Richard.

They pushed the door open wider.

They tore down the path. Emily could feel the snow crunching under her feet.

At the end of the path she touched the telephone pole.

Then she ran back to the door. She pulled at the knob.

"Hey," she said. It didn't turn.

She shivered. The door was locked.

"Yikes," said Richard. "Let me try that."

Together they pulled.

Emily could feel the wind. It tore at her blue sweat suit.

She peered through the window in the door.

Two little kids were walking down the hall.

They were carrying trays of milk.

"Here come the kindergarten snack monitors," Richard said.

Emily banged on the door.

The kindergarten kids looked at her.

One of them nearly dropped the tray.

They hurried past.

Emily shivered again.

"Maybe we should run to the front door," Richard said.

Just then someone else walked down the hall.

"I think it's a fifth grader," Emily said. She banged on the window.

"Hey," Richard said. "It's my sister, Holly."

Holly looked out. "Richard Best," she said. "Are you crazy?"

"Open the door, dummy," said Richard. "We're freezing to death out here."

Holly pushed the door open.

Emily and Richard scrambled in.

40

"Whew," Emily said. "My fingers are like icicles."

"If Mommy knew you were outside in the snow without your boots . . ." Holly said. She shook her head and started down the hall again.

Emily and Beast looked at each other.

"That was a close one," Emily said.

"We'd better get back to the classroom," Richard said.

Emily looked up.

Sherri Dent was coming down the hall toward the girls' room. She was staring at them.

Emily looked at Beast. "Come on," she said.

She didn't look at Sherri when they passed her.

They ducked into the classroom.

"Did she see us outside?" Emily asked.

"I don't know," Richard said. "Maybe."

Emily sat down in her seat.

She was still freezing. Her feet were soaked.

She pulled her sweat suit sleeves down over her hands a little.

She pulled out her notebook.

Something fell out of her desk.

It was Sherri's note. **YOU'LL BE SORRY.**

Emily shivered a little. Suppose Sherri knew?

She began to make math sticks again.

Chapter 7

After school Emily helped Timothy wash the blackboard.

She was glad school was over for today.

She was glad Ms. Rooney hadn't found out.

Emily had watched Sherri all afternoon.

She had waited for Sherri to raise her hand.

Emily made a big wet swirl with the sponge.

Sherri probably didn't know they were outside.

Of course she didn't.

Emily had been worrying over nothing.

She made a big wet *N* for *Nothing* on the chalkboard.

After Timothy left, she stopped to make a Valentine card. A special one for Jill Simon.

Jill had been absent all week.

Emily tried to rhyme with *cold*.

Last time Jill had a cold her nose was red as a beet.

It wouldn't be nice to remind her, though.

At last Emily wrote:

You are a good friend
Right to the end.
(Of the turm.)

She put a red star in the middle of the card.

It looked like a red nose. Maybe Jill's red nose.

Emily giggled. It would be her own secret.

She'd never tell anyone.

She walked over to the Valentine box.

She stuffed the card in.

The box was getting full.

She couldn't wait until Ms. Rooney passed the cards out. She hoped she'd get a lot.

Wouldn't it be awful if she didn't get any?

She went back to her seat.

She pulled out a piece of drawing paper.

Dear Emily, she wrote on top. Happy Valentine's Day.

She signed it Guess Who.

She put a gold star on top.

She tried to think if she was doing anything wrong.

No. Even Abraham Lincoln would want to get a Valentine card. Even if it were from himself.

Carefully Emily put the card into the box.

"I hope you're not looking at the cards," a voice said behind her.

Emily twirled around.

Sherri Dent.

"You're not supposed to be in here," Emily said.

"Neither are you," said Sherri.

"I am so," Emily said. "I washed the board. You think you know everything but you don't."

Sherri pushed her card into the box. "I know a lot more than you," she said. "You don't even know yellow vegetables."

45

"Who cares about vegetables?" Emily said.

Sherri walked to the door. "Turnip face," she said.

Emily opened her mouth. She tried to think of something to yell at Sherri.

By the time she did, Sherri was halfway down the hall.

Emily ran to the door. "Bug brain," she shouted.

Then she went back to the Valentine box.

She could see the edge of Sherri's card.

She'd like to rip it up into little pieces.

She looked at the writing on top. *To S . . .* it began.

Emily tried to think whose name began with *S*.

She pulled the card up. *To Sherri,* it said.

Sherri was writing Valentines to herself.

That big baby.

Then Emily remembered her own card.

She swallowed.

Just then Ms. Vincent came into the room. "Hi, Emily," she said. "You still here?"

Emily jumped. "I was washing the blackboard."

Ms. Vincent was carrying a stack of Valentine cards. "Someone's card is sticking out of the box."

Emily tried to look surprised. She leaned over. "It says, 'To Sherri.' "

"I guess Sherri has a lot of cards," Ms. Vincent said.

"Maybe," Emily said.

"Sherri is a lovely girl," said Ms. Vincent.

"Sometimes," Emily said.

She wondered if Ms. Vincent thought Sherri was lovelier than Emily.

"I liked the kittens on your collar yesterday," Ms. Vincent said.

Emily smiled. She wanted to ask if Ms. Vincent had seen her look-like-real fur jacket.

But Ms. Vincent started to talk again. "I have a kitten at home," she said.

"What's her name?" Emily asked.

"Jack," said Ms. Vincent.

"Jack," Emily said. She tried to look as if Jack were a wonderful name. "That's a very nice name."

"I named him after my boyfriend," Ms. Vincent said. She held out her hand.

Ms. Vincent was wearing a ring. It had a sparkly diamond in the middle.

"Beautiful," Emily said.

"I'm getting married in April," Ms. Vincent said. "April twenty-eighth."

"Are you having a flower girl?" Emily asked.

"I don't have any nieces," Ms. Vincent said. She smiled. "Sherri asked me that too."

Emily wondered if Sherri had asked to be the flower girl. She probably had.

Ms. Vincent started to stuff some Valentine cards into the box.

Emily could see Sherri Dent in a long pink dress.

She was marching down the aisle. She had a basket of flowers in her hand.

"Whew," said Ms. Vincent. "There's hardly any room."

"That's because people are writing Valentines to themselves," Emily said. "People like Sherri Dent."

Ms. Vincent's mouth opened.

"I have to go now," Emily said. She pulled on her jacket.

She raced out the door before Ms. Vincent could say a word.

Chapter 8

Emily and Beast rushed down the hall.

They slid into the classroom and hung up their coats.

A substitute teacher was standing in front of the room. The one with the fat body and skinny little legs.

It was Mrs. Miller. Miller the killer.

"Ms. Rooney is sick today," said Mrs. Miller. "She'll be back tomorrow."

"Yucks," Emily whispered to Beast.

She sat down at her desk.

It was going to be a horrible day.

Emily looked back over her shoulder.

Ms. Vincent was sitting next to the science table.

She winked at Emily.

51

Emily wanted to wink back.

She still had trouble with winking, though.

Both eyes winked at once.

Instead, she smiled at Ms. Vincent.

She hoped Ms. Vincent didn't remember the things she had said yesterday.

The things about Sherri Dent.

She didn't want Ms. Vincent to think she was mean.

Just then Sherri came in the door.

Mrs. Miller looked at her watch. "You're late," she told Sherri.

Sherri ducked her head. "I slept late," she said.

Good, Emily thought.

She had a mean feeling in her chest.

"Is everybody here?" Mrs. Miller asked. She looked around and counted.

"I think so," Ms. Vincent said. "Yes."

"Before we begin the boardwork," Mrs. Miller began, and frowned. "Some very serious news."

Emily looked up.

She made a serious face.

It was too bad Ms. Vincent couldn't see it.

Mrs. Miller shook her head. "Some children were outside during school yesterday."

Emily felt her face get hot.

Her heart began to pound.

"Out in the snow," Mrs. Miller said. "Without jackets or hats."

"How did you find out?" Beast asked.

"A neighbor saw them," Mrs. Miller said.

"Oh," said Beast.

Emily watched him bend over his desk. He began to draw another groundhog.

"We are trying to find out who the children are," said Mrs. Miller.

Emily looked around the room.

She made believe she was looking for the children.

Everyone else was looking around too.

Suddenly she heard Sherri take a deep breath.

Sherri's hand shot up in the air.

Dawn Bosco raised her hand too. So did Linda Lorca and Beast.

"Yes, young man?" Mrs. Miller asked Richard.

"What will happen to the children?" he asked. "Will they be left back? Or . . ."

Mrs. Miller clicked her tongue against her teeth. "We won't get into that right now."

Mrs. Miller looked around. "What is it?" she asked Dawn Bosco.

"Maybe they'll get sick," Dawn said. "You can ask all the people who stay home."

"Good idea," Emily said. She was never absent.

"That's a ridiculous idea," Mrs. Miller said.

Emily looked at Sherri out of the corner of her eye. Sherri was waving her arm back and forth.

"Well?" Mrs. Miller looked at Linda Lorca.

"You could call the FBI," said Linda.

"Or the police," said Timothy Barbiero.

Mrs. Miller rolled her eyes up to the ceiling.

"I've never heard anything so silly. The police are very busy."

"That's good," said Beast.

"Emily's father is a cop," Dawn Bosco said. "Maybe he could—"

Emily shook her head fast. "He's busy. Very busy."

"We'd better do the boardwork," Mrs. Miller said. "We're wasting time."

Sherri Dent stood up. "Emily's feet were wet," she burst out. "Yesterday. Soaking wet."

"Boardwork," said Mrs. Miller.

"It was Emily," said Sherri. "I bet anything. I even saw her in the hall. Right near the door."

"There must be a hundred people with wet feet," Mrs. Miller said.

She marched back to her desk. "A hundred people in the hall too."

"But—" Sherri began.

"Boardwork," Mrs. Miller yelled.

Emily opened her notebook.

She began to copy the board story.

It was all about winter and catching colds.

Emily sniffed a little.

She'd hate to catch a cold now.

Everyone would know she was the one who had gone outside.

Emily looked at Sherri.

Sherri was tearing a piece of paper out of her notebook. It made a loud ripping sound.

Mrs. Miller looked up. "What are you doing?"

Sherri ducked her head.

"Well?" asked Mrs. Miller.

"I'm writing a note," Sherri said. "It's to Ms. Rooney."

Beast looked back at Emily.

Emily's eyes opened wide.

She knew just what Sherri was writing.

That mean Sherri Dent.

Chapter 9

It was time to go home.

Emily went to the coatroom.

Ms. Vincent tapped her on the arm. "Tomorrow's Valentine's Day," she said.

Emily nodded.

Tomorrow Sherri would give the note to Ms. Rooney, she thought.

"We could make a card for Ms. Rooney," Ms. Vincent said. "After school."

"That would be nice." Emily tried to smile.

Everyone was lining up.

Emily went to the science table to wait.

Maybe Ms. Rooney would send her to the office tomorrow, she thought.

The class would open the Valentine box.

She wouldn't even be there to get her cards.

She wished she could tell someone. She wished she knew what to do.

Maybe she could tell Ms. Vincent.

She looked over at Sherri.

Sherri was taking a long time to get ready.

Emily wished she'd hurry.

Mrs. Miller led the line out the door.

"I'll be right back," Ms. Vincent said. "I'm going to the art room." She smiled at Emily.

Yes, Emily thought. She'd tell Ms. Vincent.

"It's time to go home," she said to Sherri.

Sherri put her nose in the air. "I have to do something."

"What?"

Sherri didn't answer.

Emily looked at Drake and Harry, the class fish. She made believe Sherri wasn't even there.

Just then Ms. Vincent came back. She had pink paper in her hand.

"Is that for the card?" Sherri asked.

Emily looked at Sherri. "How do you know about the card?"

Sherri made a pointy face. "I'm the one who's making it. Ms. Vincent asked me."

"I asked you both," said Ms. Vincent. She smiled at them.

Emily leaned against the science table.

It was hard to swallow.

The whole card idea was spoiled.

And now she'd have no time to tell Ms. Vincent.

She wished Sherri Dent were a hundred miles away.

"How will we start?" asked Ms. Vincent.

Emily tried to think of something fast.

Faster than Sherri.

"I know," Sherri said. "We could say, 'You are a good teacher.' "

"Good," said Ms. Vincent. "Write that on top."

Emily watched Sherri write across the top of the card. Her letters were big and wiggly.

"It's a little wiggly," Sherri said. "I hope I didn't spoil it."

Emily opened her mouth.

"Ms. Rooney will love it," said Ms. Vincent. "Right, Emily?"

Emily gave a little nod. Ms. Rooney would hate it, she thought.

"Your turn, Emily," said Ms. Vincent.

Emily thought. "I can't think of anything to rhyme with *teacher*," she said.

Sherri put her hand to her mouth. "I forgot it was a poem."

Emily closed her eyes. "Feacher, meacher."

"Beacher," said Sherri. "Reacher, leacher, skeacher." She took a breath. "Deacher, double feature."

Emily smiled a little. "Peacher," she said.

Then she made believe she was coughing.

She wouldn't smile at anything Sherri said.

"We could turn the paper over," said Ms. Vincent. "Start over."

Sherri picked up the Magic Marker. "This time I won't say teacher."

She wrote:

Dear Ms. Rooney. You are good.

"That will be easier," Ms. Vincent said.

Emily tried to think. "Good," she said. "Stood. Wood."

"Good like a piece of wood," said Sherri.

"No good," said Emily.

Sherri started to giggle.

"Hood," said Sherri. "Good like Red Riding Hood."

Emily looked down at the card. She thought about Ms. Rooney in a red hood.

She tried not to laugh.

Ms. Vincent stood up. "I'll get more paper."

"Ms. Rooney in a red hood," Emily said. "Or Mrs. Miller."

"No. Mrs. Miller is the big bad wolf," said Sherri. "With a big fat stomach."

Emily tried to keep her mouth closed tight.

She had forgotten that Sherri was a funny girl sometimes.

"How come you wouldn't play with me in the yard that day?" Sherri asked suddenly.

Emily stopped laughing. "I wanted to play by myself. How come you always tell on me?"

"You told on me about the big blue book," Sherri said.

Emily opened her eyes wide. She had forgotten about the big blue book.

"That was mean," Sherri said.

"I guess so," Emily said. "But what about the note to Ms. Rooney?"

"Who said I'd give the note to Ms. Rooney?" Sherri said. "I can't even find it anymore."

Just then Ms. Vincent came back into the room. "Were you two laughing in here?"

Sherri nodded a little.

So did Emily.

"That's good," said Ms. Vincent. "Sometimes fights start over silly things. They get worse and worse."

"You knew we were fighting?" Emily asked.

Ms. Vincent smiled. "I knew if you got together, you'd work it out."

She held up the pink paper. "This is the last piece."

"We'd better do it right," Emily said.

They tried to think.

"I know," Emily said. She picked up the Magic Marker.

You teach great.
The best in the state.

She gave the Magic Marker to Sherri. "Sign 'Guess Who.' "

"Whew," said Ms. Vincent.

"Whew," said Sherri.

Emily grinned.

"Hey," she said. "I forgot. I have to stop at the A&P for cupcake mix."

She dashed to the coatroom.

She grabbed her jacket.

"See you tomorrow," she yelled.

Halfway to the A&P she thought about being outside.

She had a heavy feeling in her chest.

Ms. Rooney might still find out.

She probably would.

Chapter 10

It was Valentine's Day.

Under her jacket Emily wore her pink party dress.

She carried a huge box in her arms.

She stopped in front of the A&P.

She wanted to wait for Beast.

First his sister, Holly crossed the street.

Then Emily saw Beast. He was running along on top of the snow piles.

He stopped when he saw her.

"What do you have?" he asked.

"Pink cupcakes," said Emily. "Red sprinkles."

"Too bad we couldn't eat one now," Beast said.

"Open the edge of the box," Emily said. "I made an extra one."

Beast reached into the box. "Want half?"

Emily shook her head. "Yesterday I found out I'm a tattletale. Just as bad as Sherri Dent."

"She's not so bad," Beast said.

"No," said Emily. "She's funny sometimes."

Beast bit the top off the cupcake. "Let's go," he said.

"I'm still worried," said Emily. "Worried about being outside in the snow."

They crossed the street.

"I forgot all about that," he said. He put the rest of the cupcake in his mouth.

"Maybe we should tell Ms. Rooney," Emily said.

"I was left back once already," Beast said.

They opened the big brown doors.

They were the first ones in the classroom.

Emily put the cupcake box on Ms. Rooney's desk.

She reached into her pocket. She put some cards into the Valentine box. It was really full now.

Beast went to his seat.

"I'm going to draw a George Washington," he said.

"I'm sick of worrying about being outside," Emily said.

Beast held up a crayon. "My white crayon has black things on it," he said. "I can't draw George Washington's hair."

Emily pointed to her cubby. "Take my white crayon."

She went back to her seat.

Beast bent over his paper. "George Washington never told a lie," he said.

"That was Honest Abe," said Emily.

"No," said Beast. "It was George Washington too. He chopped down a cherry tree. Then he tattled on himself."

"That's what we should do," Emily said.

The door opened. It was Ms. Rooney. "Happy Valentine's Day," she said.

Ms. Rooney pulled off one boot.

Emily looked at Beast.

He nodded. "We did something bad," she told Ms. Rooney.

"Yes," said Beast.

Emily took a breath. "We were the ones."

"Which ones?" asked Ms. Rooney.

"The ones outside in the snow," said Beast.

"Oh, yes," said Ms. Rooney. "Mrs. Miller left me a note about that."

Nobody said anything for a moment.

Emily could hear the kids in the hall.

"I'm not going to do stuff like that anymore," Emily said.

Ms. Rooney looked at Beast. "You too?"

"Me too," he said. "I'm going to be like Honest Abe and George Washington."

Ms. Rooney pulled off her other boot. "I'm glad to hear it."

She went to her desk.

Emily sat down. She took a deep breath.

71

Ms. Rooney opened the box of cupcakes. "You're a good cook, Emily."

Emily reached into her desk. One star was left.

She had to make another Valentine card.

One for Sherri Dent.

She took out a red crayon.

Here's a Valentine star.

She tried to think of a rhyme for *star*.

She was sick of rhyming.

She stuck the star on top and wrote Guess Who on the bottom.

Then she went to the Valentine box. She stuffed the card in.

Sherri would love it.

Emily couldn't wait for Valentine's Day to begin.

She hoped she'd get a pile of cards.

DON'T MISS THE LATEST
Newbery Honor Book
by beloved author
PATRICIA REILLY GIFF

It is the summer of 1944 and World War II has changed almost everyone's life. Although Lily and her grandmother are at the family's cozy house on the Atlantic Ocean, Lily's summer does not appear promising. Her father has been sent overseas and her best friend has moved to a wartime factory town. But then Lily meets Albert, a refugee from Hungary with a secret sewn into his coat. When they join together to rescue and care for a kitten, they begin a very special friendship—but one that soon becomes threatened by lies.

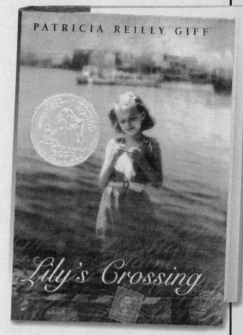

0-385-32142-2

Now available from Delacorte Press

Travel Fun with the Polk Street Kids on Tour

Join them as they take to the road to see America. Each fun-filled story includes a kid's guide to the city featuring the best attractions, museums, monuments, maps, and more!

Available from Yearling Books